The Do-Over Day

Julia Inserro   Miro Tartan

It was tuck-in time. "You're deep in thought, Layla," Grandma said.

"I'm just thinking about today. I need a do-over day."

"You want to do the day all over again?" asked Grandma.

"Oh, no! It means you get to do things differently. Mom has do-overs all the time. It's for when things don't go well. You try to have a better day tomorrow."

"That sounds really smart," said Grandma. "What went wrong today?"

"Well, first I had to get up early even though it was Saturday.
Mac used my favorite cup at breakfast,
and the maple syrup touched my strawberries."

"Then Nina used all my favorite socks on her octopus
so I had to wear plain white."

"Mom said I couldn't wear my mermaid costume to the dentist...

... and at the dentist, Nina got to push the elevator button first!"

DENTIST
Floor 1

"Mac and Nina got to ride in the grocery cart and pretend they were flying and I had to hold onto the side. The store was all out of O-Tee-Os so we got Nina's favorite Wheatie-Bees. Yuck."

"Nina's window was down more than mine.
And Mom said we didn't need to get any donuts
even after I told her that it was Secret Donut Saturday."

"Mrs. McCarver said I wasn't allowed to wear my rain boots for ballet class!"

"Coco stole my pencil and Mom said I had to include
Nina and Mac when I played Cupcake Maze,
even though they play it wrong."

"After that, Dad said I couldn't use his tools
and Mac and Nina got to lick the cookie batter bowl.
I only got the spoon."

"And then Mom said I couldn't eat nine cookies, even though she knows that nine is my favorite number of all time."

"Dad questioned whether I actually used soap
to clean my hands ...

... and he said I couldn't wear my
snorkel and fins in the bathtub."

"Mom told me I couldn't wear my tutu to bed.
Nina chose Pink Prancing Ponies for a bedtime story
even though she chooses it every single night.
And Coco wanted to sleep with Mac instead of me."

Grandma sat quietly and held Layla's hand.
Then she said, "You have quite the memory.
That's a lot to deal with. So, what would you
do differently in your do-over day?"

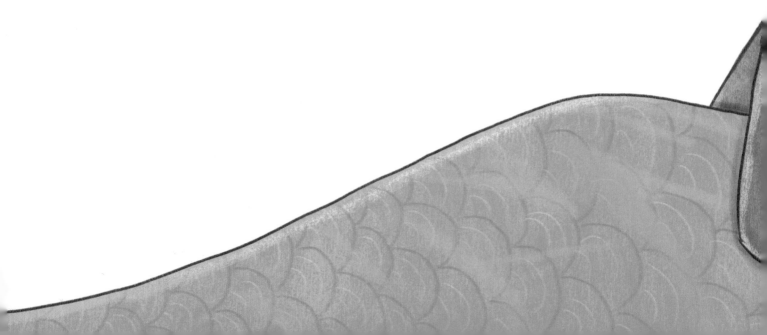

Layla thought for a moment.

"I guess it would be difficult to wear my mermaid costume in the car. And maybe wearing rain boots would make it hard to pirouette. Nina really does love pushing elevator buttons, so we could take turns," said Layla.

"Those are great ideas!" said Grandma.

"And maybe I could just wear my snorkel in the bath and use the fins at the beach."

Grandma smiled.

"You know, sometimes I have bad days, too," said Grandma.
"Do you think I can have a do-over day as well?"

Layla smiled. "Definitely. Everyone can have a do-over day."

"Good night, my love," said Grandma.

"Good night, Grandma. I love you.
Now I'm excited about having my do-over day."

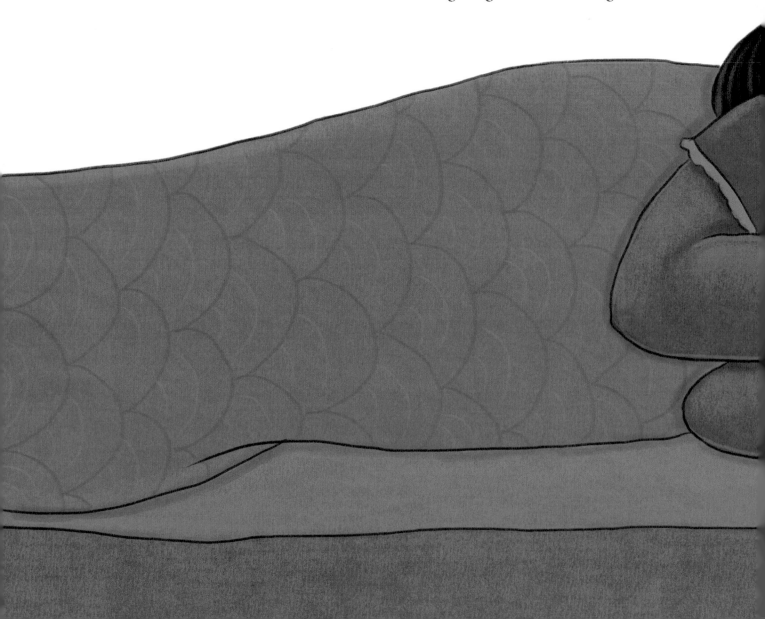

Do you ever have a bad day?
Nothing goes right? Want to know what I do?
I think about what happened.
I think about how it made me feel.
And I think about how I acted.
Then I try to think how I could do it differently
next time, when I get my do-over day.
Why don't you try it?

EVENT - My sister chose the TV show tonight

THINK - My sister always gets to choose!
FEEL - Angry
ACT - I pout and act all mopey.
-OR-
THINK - My sister got to choose the TV show tonight.
FEEL - Grateful that I get to watch TV.
ACT - Thankful that tomorrow it's my choice.

EVENT - My brother plays with my toy.

THINK - That's my toy! He didn't even ask to borrow it.
FEEL - Frustrated
ACT - Go and grab toy back and tell him he can never ever play with it again – EVER!
-OR-
THINK – That's my toy! He didn't even ask to borrow it.
FEEL - Disappointed
ACT - Ask him to ask me first next time, but let him play with it now.

EVENT - My friend got a gift.

THINK - My friend got new shoes and I didn't get anything.
FEEL - Jealous
ACT - Refuse to play with them and sulk in my room.

-OR-

THINK - My friend got new shoes and I didn't get anything.
FEEL - Excited
ACT - Ask them to play and see how fast they can run.

EVENT - My sandwich is cut into squares.

THINK - Mom forgot that I only eat my sandwiches in triangles.
FEEL - Sad
ACT - I cry and refuse to eat lunch.

-OR-

THINK - Mom forgot that I like to eat my sandwiches cut into triangles.
FEEL - Unhappy (and hungry)
ACT - I can eat square sandwiches today and help Mom make my lunch for tomorrow.

Can you think of more examples?

EVENT - I forgot my gym shoes today.

THINK - I might get in trouble for not having my gym shoes.
FEEL - Anxious and worried
ACT - I cry and hide in the bathroom.

-OR-

THINK - I might get in trouble for not having my gym shoes.
FEEL - Upset and uncertain.
ACT - Ask my teacher what we can do and borrow some shoes or call home.

Check out **WWW.JULIAINSERRO.COM** for freebies and book updates.
And don't forget to grab these other books by Julia Inserro.

Dedicated to L, M and N, who often need a do-over day, and who readily remind me that mommies need do-over days, too. - JI

For G, A and C. I'd never want to have a do-over day without my three musketeers. - MT

Author: Julia Inserro (www.juliainserro.com)
Illustrator: Miro Tartan (www.miroillo.com)
Printed in the United States of America
First Printing, 2019
ISBN 978-1-947891-06-7

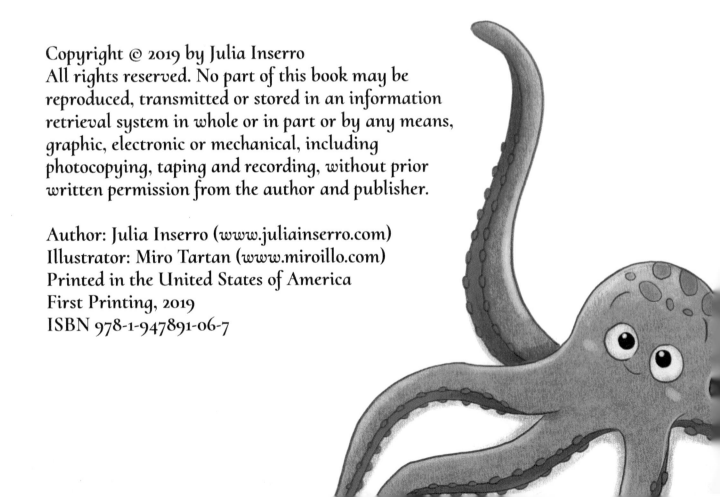

Made in the USA
Las Vegas, NV
06 December 2020